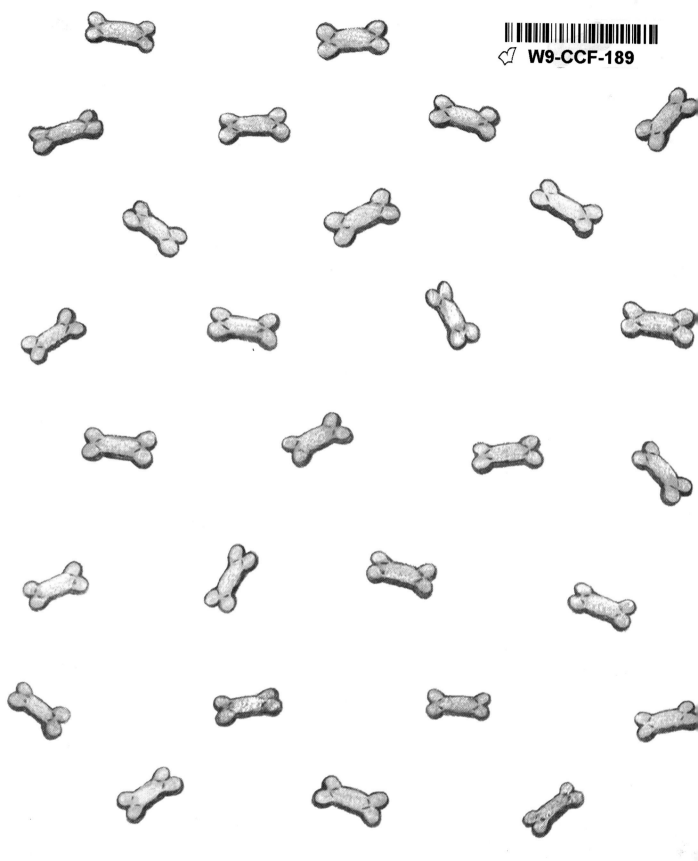

Typography by Tom Starace
1   2   3   4   5   6   7   8   9   10
❖
First Edition

Biscuit's Picnic

story by ALYSSA SATIN CAPUCILLI
pictures by PAT SCHORIES

HarperCollins*Publishers*

"Biscuit, where are you?"
called the little girl.

Woof, woof!

"Silly puppy! What are you doing under there?"
Woof!

"I'm sorry, Biscuit. This picnic is just for kids.
You and Puddles can run and play."

Bow wow!
Woof, woof!
"Go on, puppies. Go and play!"

"Wait, Biscuit! Come back, Puddles!
Where are you going with that food?"

Tweet, tweet, tweet.

"Look!" The little girl laughed.
"Biscuit and Puddles are having
their own picnic—

and the birds want
to join them."

Bow wow!
Woof, woof, woof!

Meow.

"Even Daisy wants to have a picnic!"

Meow.

Woof, woof!

Bow wow, bow wow!

"Careful, Biscuit!" said the little girl.
"Watch out for the—

—CAKE!"

"Biscuit is covered in cake!"
 the little boy giggled.
"Oh, Biscuit," said the little girl.
"What do we do now?"

Woof, woof!

"Funny puppy. You're right, Biscuit," she said.
"We can all have a picnic together!"

Woof!

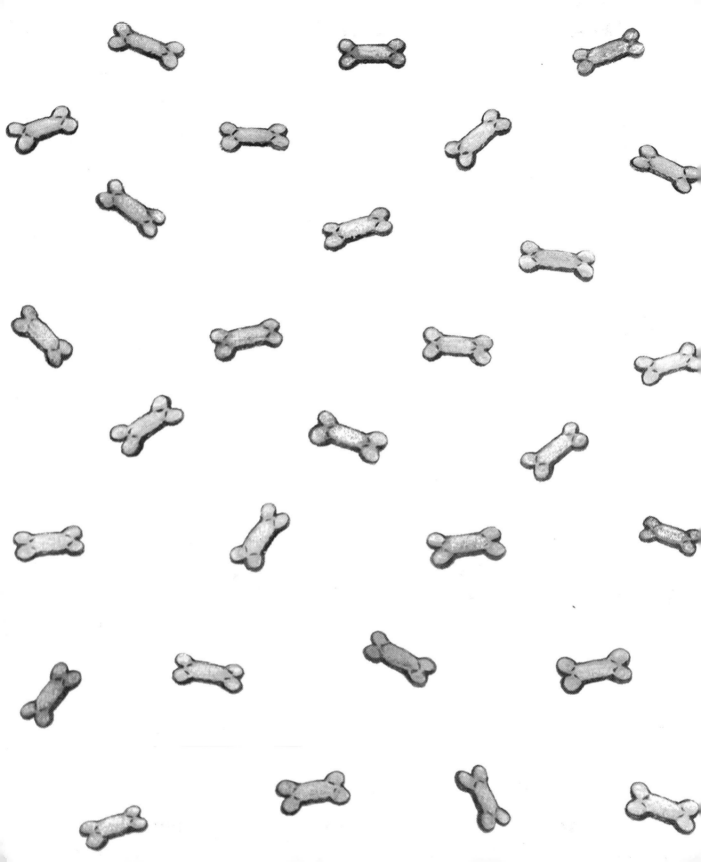